SKELETON CREEK
IS REAL

By Patrick Carman

Recent statements made by yours truly, Patrick Carman, the writer of this book:

2011
I wrote a book called Skeleton Creek. It is a work of fiction.

2012
Some of what skeletoncreekisreal.com says is true. Not all of it, but some of it. That's all I have to say on the subject.

2013
There were things that happened during the making of Skeleton Creek that I am not at liberty to share. Maybe someday, but not today.

2014
Urban legends are as real as our imaginations choose to make them.

I think I'll use journal entries

Ryan McCray, the fictional character I created for the Skeleton Creek series, was big on keeping a journal. He told the whole story of four books in his own voice, and when there are more Skeleton Creek stories to tell, it will be Ryan who tells them. So I think it's only appropriate that I use the same process here.

I don't know if you'll like my voice as well as you do Ryan's, but I'll try to keep it interesting. Really I will. And I think if you can stay with me to the end, you'll be surprised at how this all turns out. I think it will be worth your time.

These journal entries will be combined with many videos you'll need to go online and watch, something you already

KNOW HOW TO DO IF YOU'VE EVER READ A SKELETON CREEK BOOK. IF BY SOME STRANGE CHANCE YOU HAVE NEVER READ A SKELETON CREEK BOOK AND YOU'RE READING THIS NOW, YOU MAY WANT TO FAMILIARIZE YOURSELF WITH THE SERIES BY WATCHING THE TRAILER VIDEO.

HERE'S WHERE YOU STOP READING, SET THE BOOK DOWN, AND GO ONLINE TO WATCH A VIDEO.

YOU'LL ALWAYS GO HERE TO WATCH:
WWW.SARAHFINCHER.COM

AND YOU'LL ALWAYS ENTER A PASSWORD.

SARAHFINCHER.COM

PASSWORD:

TRAILER

This book will have many breaks along the way to watch part of the story, so many in fact that you might want to keep a computer or a tablet nearby. It will also include entries made by the person who claims Skeleton Creek is real, along with comments and theories from readers just like you. I'll tell you what I think after each and every piece of evidence, but you'll need to decide for yourself if Skeleton Creek is real.

This book might be even more interesting than a true work of fiction. And we both know why that is: some of what's in this book could actually be true.

So why am I writing this book when I could be writing a novel?

Maybe you're someone who doesn't believe in ghosts or spirits or conspiracies about hidden aliens living among us. I would say I fall into that camp, but the longer I'm alive and the more I see, the less sure I am about any of it.

I'm writing this book because someone went to a lot of trouble to prove the story of Skeleton Creek was not a work of fiction I made up in my head, but an actual story I stumbled onto. They say I altered the story I was told in order to hide the truth.

I have every shred of evidence that was gathered to make this case. A lot of it is in video form. Some of it might shock you. But I promise you this: if you make it to the end of this book, it will change

THE WAY YOU FEEL ABOUT SKELETON CREEK. AND WHAT I REVEAL AT THE END WILL BLOW YOUR MIND.

HEY, HOW'D YOU GET YOUR HANDS ON THIS STUFF?

HOW DID I END UP IN POSSESSION OF ALL THE VIDEOS AND OTHER ASSETS FROM THE FORMER SKELETON CREEK IS REAL SITE? I STRUCK A DEAL WITH THE PERSON WHO CREATED THIS URBAN LEGEND, WITH THE PROMISE THAT I WOULD NOT REVEAL HIS IDENTITY. IN RETURN, HE AGREED TO RELINQUISH HIS HOLD ON THE WEB SITE AND THE MATERIAL HOUSED THERE. A DEAL IS A DEAL — I'LL TELL HIS STORY AND COMMENT ON IT AS I GO, AND I WON'T REVEAL WHO HE IS.

FOR THE PURPOSES OF THIS JOURNAL, I'M GOING TO REFER TO THE PERSON-WHO-SHALL-NOT-BE-NAMED AS PAUL CHANDLER.

It's the fake name they asked me to use, and it will be easier to understand if I'm not always saying 'the person who made this material blah blah blah' — so Paul Chandler it is.

The unreliable narrator strikes again

Do you know what an unreliable narrator is? Probably you do, just like you know a fake name is also known as a pseudonym. But in case it's slipped your mind, an unreliable narrator is someone telling a story, only it's hard to know whether or not they're telling the truth.

The first book I ever read with an unreliable narrator that really grabbed me was The Turn of the Screw by Henry James. In that book, the narrator tells a haunted tale that seems very

REAL, BUT IN THE END, YOU REALIZE SHE WAS PROBABLY CRAZY ALL ALONG. THE NARRATOR WAS LYING. BUT IT'S TRICKY, BECAUSE SHE NEVER COMES OUT AND SAYS SHE WAS LYING. SOMEWHERE ALONG THE WAY I STOPPED TRUSTING HER.

A FEW RECENT BOOKS YOU MAY HAVE HEARD OF THAT HAVE UNRELIABLE NARRATORS INCLUDE GONE GIRL, SHUTTER ISLAND, AND LIFE OF PI.

YOU MAY FIND, IN THE END, THAT OUR YOUNG MAN PAUL CHANDLER HAS THE SCENT OF UNRELIABILITY. OR YOU MAY DECIDE THAT IT'S ME, THE WRITER OF THIS JOURNAL, WHO CANNOT BE TRUSTED. POSSIBLY IT WILL BE A COMBINATION OF THE TWO. ONLY YOU CAN DECIDE WHO AND WHAT YOU BELIEVE.

WALK WITH ME NOW, LET'S TALK ABOUT THIS

THING WE CALL AN URBAN LEGEND.

IS IT A HOTDOG OR A DOUGHNUT?
SO WHAT THE HECK IS AN URBAN LEGEND?
IS IT THE TRUTH OR A LIE? IS IT REAL
OR IMAGINED? I LIKE TO THINK AN URBAN
LEGEND IS ALWAYS SOME COMBINATION OF
BOTH. UNLIKE A HOTDOG, WHICH IS ALWAYS
A HOTDOG; OR A DOUGHNUT, WHICH IS ALWAYS
A DOUGHNUT, AN URBAN LEGEND IS A SHIFTY
LITTLE SOMETHING THAT REFUSES TO REMAIN
THE SAME THING TO EVERYONE.

AN URBAN LEGEND IS A STORY THAT THE
TELLER MAY OR MAY NOT BELIEVE IS TRUE.
IF THE STORY IS GOOD ENOUGH, THEN TRUE OR
FALSE, IT STANDS ON ITS OWN MERITS. IT GETS
TOLD AGAIN. AND AGAIN. AND FOR REASONS
WE CAN NEVER REALLY KNOW, AN URBAN
LEGEND STAYS IN CIRCULATION OVER TIME.
IT GAINS SOME KIND OF POWER OF ITS OWN.

It shifts and moves from its center, but always it's there.

Obviously, based on this definition, I would not be a good dictionary writer. Which is fine by me because writing the dictionary sounds boring.

When I was a teenager growing up in Salem, Oregon it was the 1980's. The urban legends that grabbed us back then were The Amityville Horror, about a house we all believed was truly haunted. There were stories of alien sightings, even television specials that examined all the evidence. And of course there was Sasquatch, the half man half ape who lived in the woods and kidnapped children.

I remember one particularly scary urban legend that was told to me at summer camp. It was called the Atomic Ants, and it made it into a short story I wrote. At this camp I went to, there was an old concrete drain cover about a hundred yards away from the main area. One day a counselor took me and my buddies out there and showed it to us. It was big, like twice the size of a manhole cover, and really heavy. It looked too heavy to move.

This counselor told us that an experiment had taken place back in the sixties that involved ants and nuclear waste. Under that heavy concrete drain cover, those ants still existed. They were bigger than he was. He was a big guy so these were, apparently, gigantic ants. We didn't believe him.

Or did we?

The next day I found myself telling the same story to a group of other kids. They didn't believe me so I took them out into the woods to show them the evidence. When I got there, the concrete cover had been moved. I promise with all that is in me I could hear the sound of giant, man eating ants moving around down there. The legend grew.

My own kids believe the abandoned cemetery on a farming road outside of Walla Walla is haunted. They say ghosts have been sighted up there. They keep their own urban legend going.

I hear young people talking about Slender Man these days, and it reminds me how powerful urban legends can be (you wait, that tall shadowy dude will get his own movie).

I STILL THINK THE ATOMIC ANTS ARE REAL.
I THINK THE AMITYVILLE HOUSE IS HAUNTED.
MY IMAGINATION WON'T LET ME BELIEVE
OTHERWISE.

AND SO WE BEGIN

LET'S GET DOWN TO BUSINESS! THE QUESTION
AT HAND IS SIMPLE: IS SKELETON CREEK
REAL?

EXHIBIT A IS THE SITE PAUL CHANDLER BUILT,
WHERE HE CHRONICLED HIS BELIEF THAT THE
STORY TOLD IN SKELETON CREEK WAS IN
FACT TRUE.

THE SITE CONTAINED THE FOLLOWING

MATERIAL:
14 VIDEOS.
A SERIES OF BLOG ENTRIES.
OVER 30,000 COMMENTS FROM PEOPLE
JUST LIKE YOU.

Hundreds of theories about what was really going on.
A list of Easter eggs, or hidden files associated with the books.

While that site has been taken down and replaced with the videos for this book, Paul did create a video that showed what it once looked like. He included it with all the other files, so you can see for yourself what once was.

Take a moment now to view a series of images that made up the notorious Skeleton Creek is Real site.

SARAHFINCHER.COM

PASSWORD:

SASQUATCH

And now we turn our attention to the videos themselves, the core of the legend.

Video number one

The videos on Skeletoncreekisreal.com were organized from beginning to end to tell a story. I'm going to present each of those videos in order. After each video, I'll comment on what we've both just seen.

The first video MUST be watched before you continue reading or you won't understand my comments about it.

www.sarahfincher.com
password: suspicion1941

First off let me say I love the music, so much so that I used it as the theme for

THIS PROJECT. IT'S CHILLING AND UNSETTLING, BUT IT'S ALSO GOT A SOOTHING QUALITY TO IT. VERY NICE! THIS VIDEO IS THE FIRST INSTANCE WHERE ACTUAL FOOTAGE FROM THE PROJECT WAS SAMPLED. THAT SCENE WHERE SARAH FINDS THE DREDGE FOR THE FIRST TIME ALSO APPEARS IN ONE OF THE FIRST SKELETON CREEK VIDEOS.

LET ME TALK A LITTLE BIT ABOUT THAT PARTICULAR SNIPPET OF VIDEO. IT WASN'T SHOT AT THE DREDGE, WHERE WE DID MOST OF OUR INTERIOR SHOTS. GO BACK AND WATCH THE VIDEO AGAIN AND YOU'LL SEE THAT THE BUILDING DOESN'T MATCH UP WITH WHAT THE ACTUAL DREDGE REALLY LOOKS LIKE. THERE'S A REASON FOR THAT: THE FOOTAGE FOR THIS EXTERIOR VIEW WAS SHOT ELSEWHERE.

I REMEMBER THAT NIGHT WELL. IT WAS

REALLY LATE AND IT WAS COLD. I THINK WE MUST HAVE BEEN SHOOTING IN THE EARLY WINTER OF 2008. THE REASON WE SHOT THIS OUTSIDE FOOTAGE OF THE DREDGE HERE, ALONG WITH THAT ICONIC IMAGE OF THE GHOST OF OLD JOE BUSH IN THE WINDOW, WAS BECAUSE THE ACTUAL DREDGE SITS ON A POND. IT WAS IMPOSSIBLE TO GET IN CLOSE ENOUGH TO SHOOT WHAT WE WANTED.

HERE'S THE REALLY SCARY PART ABOUT THAT PIECE OF VIDEO AND WHY I FIND IT SO INTERESTING THAT IT IS THIS PARTICULAR PIECE THAT WAS USED AT THE VERY BEGINNING OF PAUL CHANDLER'S STORY: WITHIN A YEAR OF US FILMING THERE, THE LOCATION BURNED TO THE GROUND. IT WAS A HISTORICAL LANDMARK IN WAITSBURG, WASHINGTON CALLED THE WAIT'S MILL. THE THING WAS BIG, AND WHEN I SAY IT BURNED TO THE GROUND, I MEAN THAT FIRE BASICALLY TURNED THE WHOLE THING

INTO A PILE OF ASHES. LOOK IT UP ONLINE, YOU'LL SEE FOR YOURSELF.

COINCIDENCE? MAYBE. BUT IT ALWAYS STRUCK ME AS STRANGE THAT THIS MILL STOOD FOR OVER A HUNDRED YEARS, THEN WE BRING THE GHOST OF OLD JOE BUSH INTO IT AND THE WHOLE THING GOES UP IN FLAMES.

SOMETHING ELSE WORTH MENTIONING: THIS VIDEO OF PAUL'S APPEARED ONLINE BEFORE THE FIRST SKELETON CREEK BOOK CAME OUT. PAUL SAYS HE KNOWS ABOUT THE BOOK. HE HAS FOOTAGE THAT HADN'T BEEN RELEASED TO THE PUBLIC. AND HE CLAIMS THE STORY I'M TELLING IN THIS BOOK THAT HASN'T COME OUT YET IS NOT MADE UP. IT'S REAL.

SO HOW DID OUR PAUL CHANDLER GET THAT VIDEO? FOR THE ANSWER TO THAT QUESTION, WE HAVE TO TURN TO THE SECOND VIDEO HE

POSTED.

What's up with the weird passwords? Before we check that video, I'd like to share something with you about the passwords in this and every other Skeleton Creek project. You may have noticed that these passwords are often unusual sounding. That's by design for two reasons:

1. If you put a Skeleton Creek password into a search engine, it will send you on a path towards other iconic material I want you to know about. Most of what you'll find relates to books and movies and characters and writers that have inspired me. I want you to go find them and, in a perfect scenario, I hope you choose to explore them as far as they will take you. This is as true of

THE BOOK YOUR READING RIGHT NOW AS IT IS EVERY OTHER SKELETON CREEK STORY.

2. BUT THERE'S ANOTHER REASON FOR THESE PASSWORDS, AND IT'S HARDER TO FIGURE OUT. THE PASSWORDS, ONCE YOU UNDERSTAND WHAT THEY REFER TO, SHOULD ALWAYS GIVE YOU INSIGHT INTO WHAT I'M TRYING TO TELL YOU ABOUT MY STORY (OR PAUL'S IN THIS CASE). SO FOR EXAMPLE, IF YOU WATCH A SKELETON CREEK VIDEO AND THE PASSWORD IS THERAVEN, THEN THE RAVEN POEM BY EDGAR ALLEN POE SHOULD SOMEHOW RELATE TO THE INFORMATION YOU JUST READ AND WATCHED. IT MIGHT BE SUBTLE, BUT IT'S THERE. TRY TO CONNECT THE DOTS, BECAUSE SOMETIMES, I'M HIDING SOMETHING ONLY THOSE WHO ARE WILLING TO REALLY DIG WILL FIGURE OUT.

Video number two

Back you go to the Skeleton Creek is Real site in order to watch the second video. What I say about it won't mean much if you don't.

SARAHFINCHER.COM

PASSWORD:

UDOLPHO

FINDING PHANTOM FILES. IT'S A GOOD TITLE
FOR A VIDEO, SO PROPS THERE. WE'LL GET
TO WHAT PAUL IS REFERRING TO WITH THAT
TERM IN A SECOND, BUT I FIRST WANT TO
TALK ABOUT THE VOICE ON THESE VIDEOS. I
DID SOME CHECKING WITH AN AUDIO EXPERT
AND SHE CONFIRMED THAT THE VOICE IN
THESE VIDEOS HAS BEEN ALTERED. SO PAUL
CHANDLER FOR SURE WANTS TO PROTECT HIS
IDENTITY, EVEN FROM THE POSSIBILITY OF
SOMEONE RECOGNIZING HIS VOICE.

I THINK HE WANTS TO PROTECT HIS IDENTITY
BECAUSE HE KNOWS HE COULD GET INTO SOME
REAL TROUBLE FOR TAKING THESE FILES.
LET'S CIRCLE BACK TO THAT NOW: THE
PHANTOM FILES. PHANTOM FILES ARE A REAL
THING ON THE INTERNET. I'M CONSTANTLY
PUTTING NEW THINGS ON MY OWN SITES, AND IN
DOING THAT, PROGRAMMERS OFTEN LEAVE OLD
STUFF ONLINE IN HIDDEN DIRECTORIES. THEY

DO THIS BECAUSE IT'S EASIER TO GO BACK AND FIND STUFF THEY WANT IF IT'S WHERE THEY LEFT IT. YOUR AVERAGE WEB SURFER WOULDN'T HAVE ANY IDEA THAT THESE FILES ARE THERE, BUT A PROGRAMMER CAN EASILY FIND THEM.

AND THIS PART PAUL CHANDLER GOT RIGHT. BY BACK SLASHING THE END OF A WEB ADDRESS AND ADDING WORDS, YOU MIGHT STUMBLE ONTO HIDDEN FILES. THEY'D JUST BE SITTING THERE IN FOLDERS, UNPROTECTED. IT'S HOW HE FOUND FILES I DIDN'T EVEN REALIZE WERE ON THE WEB TO BEGIN WITH. PAUL WAS DETERMINED. HE DIDN'T TRY SEARCHING FOR OLD DIRECTORIES A FEW TIMES, HE TRIED OVER 50 TIMES.

THIS MIGHT MAKE YOU WONDER — WAS IT YOUR WEBMASTER THAT BUILT SKELETON CREEK IS REAL? HE HAD ACCESS TO

EVERYTHING AND HE WAS NEARBY FOR THE WHOLE PROJECT. MAYBE HE'S OUR PAUL CHANDLER. IT'S POSSIBLE, THAT'S ALL I'LL SAY. I'M NOT SAYING HE DID IT OR HE DIDN'T, BUT HE DEFINITELY HAD ACCESS TO A LOT OF THINGS OTHER PEOPLE DIDN'T.

BUT BACK TO THESE FILES — WHY WERE THEY STORED ON THE INTERNET TO BEGIN WITH? BACK IN 2008 I WOULD HAVE BEEN MORE LIKELY TO KEEP THAT STUFF ON MY HARD DRIVE, BUT I OFTEN PROVIDED OUR WEBMASTER WITH MORE THAN HE NEEDED, IN PART TO CREATE ARCHIVES. I DO RECALL HAVING A LOT OF VIDEO FOOTAGE I HADN'T EVEN LOOKED THROUGH YET. WE HAD HOURS AND HOURS OF VIDEO THAT NEVER GOT USED, BUT I DIDN'T WANT TO LOSE IT. PROBABLY THE FILES PAUL FOUND WERE PART OF A LARGER HAUL OF STUFF, VIDEOS THAT WERE UPLOADED FOR STORAGE AND NOTHING MORE.

The troubling thing about the six videos Paul shows in this clip is the dates on them. We shot everything for the first Skeleton Creek project in 2008. The videos Paul found? Those are dated in 2001 and 2002, more than five years prior to my even writing a Skeleton Creek book.

Yeah, so that's a little weird.

Paul also says that he checked back the next day and found that the directory he had uncovered was gone. This does add up, because however lame our security was back in those days, I do think my webmaster at the time would have known if someone had pulled these files down off our server. I do recall my webmaster mentioning we had been hacked several times over that period of time,

BUT THAT NOTHING IMPORTANT WAS TAKEN AND MY SITES HADN'T BEEN COMPROMISED. IT'S NOT UNUSUAL TO BE HACKED, IT HAPPENS A LOT. BUSINESS AS USUAL. I DIDN'T MAKE A BIG DEAL OUT OF IT.

I SHOULD ALSO MENTION HERE, BECAUSE IT'S POSSIBLY RELEVANT: THE OLDEST DATES ON THE VIDEOS PAUL FOUND WERE IN 2001. THAT WOULD HAVE PRE-DATED MY GOING UP TO THE LOCATION BY MANY YEARS AND THAT JUST DIDN'T HAPPEN. SO HERE I WOULD HAVE TO CONCLUDE THAT PAUL CHANDLER DOCTORED THOSE FILES TO MAKE THEM LOOK LIKE THEY WERE FROM AN EARLIER DATE.

I DON'T HAVE ANOTHER EXPLANATION.

Video number three

It's really getting interesting now. This was the first video I watched where I thought to myself: okay, whoever this is, they're not messing around. They're doing some serious sleuthing here.

SARAHFINCHER.COM

Password:

VATHEK

PAUL CLAIMS IN THIS VIDEO THAT THE FILES
HE FOUND AND SHOWS WERE RECORDED IN
THE SUMMER OF 2001. BUT AS I ALREADY
MENTIONED, SOME OF THAT FOOTAGE WAS SHOT
BY MY TEAM IN 2008 AT THE WAIT'S MILL
IN WASHINGTON. SO HERE WE HAVE SOMEONE
DOCTORING FILE NAMES SO IT LOOKS LIKE
THESE VIDEOS WERE MADE BEFORE THEY
ACTUALLY WERE.

IF THAT'S NOT WHAT'S HAPPENING, THEN THE
ONLY ALTERNATIVE IS THAT I'M LYING TO
YOU RIGHT NOW. MAYBE THESE FILES WERE
CREATED IN THE SUMMER OF 2001. I CAN'T
MAKE YOU BELIEVE ME, AND I CAN'T MAKE
YOU NOT BELIEVE PAUL CHANDLER. I THINK
WHEN WE GET CLOSER TO THE END IT WILL
BE EASIER TO DECIDE FOR YOURSELF.

I DO LIKE HIS QUESTIONS AT THE END OF THE
VIDEO, PARTICULARLY THIS ONE: WHY ARE

THEY HIDING THIS?

TO THAT I WOULD SAY I WASN'T HIDING
ANYTHING OTHER THAN MATERIAL FOR A BOOK
THAT HADN'T COME OUT YET.

THIS IS ONE OF THOSE TIMES WHERE I FELT A
CHILL UP MY SPINE. WHY WOULD SOMEONE GO
TO SO MUCH TROUBLE TO CREATE A FANTASY
ABOUT WHAT WAS REALLY GOING ON?

THEORY #1

PAUL CHANDLER HAD THE SITE UP AND RUNNING
FOR SEVERAL YEARS, AND DURING THAT TIME,
HE ALLOWED PEOPLE TO POST THEORIES
ABOUT WHAT THEY THOUGHT. OVER 1000
THEORIES WERE SHARED AND I'VE INCLUDED A
BROAD SAMPLING OF THOSE THEORIES IN THIS
BOOK. I'M GOING TO KEEP SOME OF THE FAN
THEORIES UNTIL THE END, BUT I'D LIKE TO
SHARE A FEW AS WE GO.

WHEN I SHOW THESE THEORIES, KEEP IN MIND
THAT I'M NOT EDITING THEM OTHER THAN
FOR SPELLING AND PUNCTUATION (SO THERE
STILL MIGHT BE SPELLING ERRORS BECAUSE
I'M A SO-SO SPELLER). THESE ARE ACTUAL
THEORIES POSTED BY REAL PEOPLE JUST
LIKE YOU. PEOPLE WHO READ THE BOOKS AND
WONDERED WHAT WAS REALLY HAPPENING.

THEORY POSTED BY ADMIRAL GREE

CHANCES ARE THIS IS ALL MADE UP BY THE
PERSON RUNNING THIS WEBSITE BUT SO FAR
I'M INCLINED TO BELIEVE HIM. PARTIALLY
BECAUSE PATRICK CARMAN'S RESPONSES
HAVEN'T BEEN THAT GREAT, BUT ALSO THE
CHANCES ARE THAT PATRICK CARMAN WAS
LOOKING FOR A GHOST STORY TO WRITE AND
SOMEHOW HE KNEW SOMEONE FROM THE AREA
WHO KNEW SOMEONE WHO KEPT A JOURNAL
THAT HAD DOCUMENTATION OF SCARY THINGS
IN THEM. I THINK HE TOOK THAT AND THE

HISTORY OF THE DREDGE AND JOE BUSH AND MADE THIS WHOLE BOOK SERIES ABOUT IT. FINDING SOMEONE LOOKING INTO HIS PRIVATE STUFF MADE HIM NERVOUS AND NOW HE WON'T TALK ABOUT IT TO ANYONE.

VIDEO NUMBER FOUR

YOU KNOW WHAT TO DO — GO WATCH THE FOURTH VIDEO, THEN LET'S BREAK IT DOWN.

SARAHFINCHER.COM

Password:

ELLISBELL

It's important to remember that at this point in the story Paul is telling, the first Skeleton Creek book hadn't come out yet. So here he's trying to piece together some things that we already know. He's trying to place the location, who these people are, and what's going on.

The video snippets Paul shows here also appear in the first Skeleton Creek book. So now you must be asking yourself: is there any chance that Patrick Carman found these videos at an earlier date and used them in his project?

This is a hard question for me to answer, because it's complicated. Most of the footage you see that relates to the first Skeleton Creek book was shot

FOR THE PROJECT, BUT NOT ALL OF IT. SOME OF IT I FOUND THROUGH RESEARCH, SOME OF IT WAS GIVEN TO ME. I'M NOT AT LIBERTY TO SAY WHAT PARTS MY TEAM MADE AND WHAT PARTS MY TEAM DID NOT MAKE. IT'S A SENSITIVE AREA.

I CAN VERIFY A FEW THINGS ABOUT WHAT HE'S SHOWING ON THIS CLIP.

1. THIS FOOTAGE IS FOR SURE FROM THE DREDGE THAT WE SHOT ON.

2. THAT THING IN THE GROUND IS A PROP WE BUILT, I WAS THERE WHEN WE CREATED IT.

3. SOME OF WHAT'S ON THIS VIDEO I DID NOT MAKE. I'M NOT AT LIBERTY TO SAY WHAT PARTS.

4: The moment where something begins to move into the screen is fantastic! It's something I remember very well. I remember creating that moment, but I also remember hearing about it from someone else. I can't recall who it was that I heard it from.

Some of the details about the years 2005 through 2010 are hard to remember exactly. There was so much going on, so many videos being reviewed and handed to me. There was some talk about video inspiration being provided from a source, but I wasn't personally shooting or editing the videos.

Is it possible that some of the material used for the first Skeleton Creek book came from content we didn't shoot? It's more than possible, it definitely

HAPPENED. I'M SIMPLY NOT GOING TO SAY WHERE THE FOOTAGE CAME FROM OR WHAT PARTS THEY MIGHT BE. I DO KNOW THAT IN SOME CASES, SKELETON CREEK VIDEOS ARE FEATHERED TOGETHER FROM MORE THAN ONE SOURCE. I CAN'T SAY ANYTHING MORE THAN THAT.

FAN THEORY POSTED BY KOGAGIRL

PATRICK CARMAN FOUND OUT THAT WE ARE FINDING STUFF OUT ON THE WEB SO HE IS TRYING TO COVER UP WHAT HE DID. HE FOUND THIS STORY. IT'S TRUE!

VIDEO NUMBER FIVE

PAUL'S FIFTH VIDEO HAS SOMETHING IN IT THAT I CAN'T EXPLAIN. IT'S A GLITCH AT THE BEGINNING OF THE VIDEO THAT FINALLY STARTED TO MAKE ME SERIOUSLY WONDER WHAT WAS HAPPENING WITH THIS SITUATION.

Take a look and then I'll tell you what
I mean.

SARAHFINCHER.COM

Password:

WOLFENBACH

Here Paul is referring to the last two video files he claims he downloaded from my server: videos 32 and 35. He claims these videos are dated April, 2002. We've already discussed the fact that Paul has no proof of when these videos were actually shot. He's just telling us April, 2002 and expecting us to believe him.

The first thing Paul describes is a section of video from the Skeleton Creek project, something I created for the series where Ryan is walking up the stairs in the dredge. But then Paul Chandler does something kind of amazing: he freezes the video at the point where there's a glitch, and in that glitch he finds something hidden. It's a picture of a girl sitting in front of a monitor, turning to her right. But the way it's captured

WE SEE THE TOP OF HER HEAD IN ONE IMAGE AND THE BOTTOM OF HER HEAD IN ANOTHER. YOU HAVE TO SEE IT TO UNDERSTAND WHAT I'M SAYING. SEVERAL THINGS ABOUT THIS IMAGE:

1. I DIDN'T SHOOT IT.

2. I DON'T KNOW WHO THIS GIRL IS.

3. I DON'T KNOW WHAT IT'S DOING HIDDEN IN ONE OF MY VIDEOS.

SO THERE ARE ONLY A FEW OPTIONS FOR WHERE THIS IMAGE CAME FROM:

1. PAUL CHANDLER PUT IT THERE IN ORDER TO ADD TO HIS STORY.

2. SOMEONE WORKING ON THE PROJECT WITH ME PUT IT THERE WITHOUT TELLING ME.

3. This is more evidence of me not knowing my own material, which would seem to support the idea that I got the videos from someone else.

4. I planted that image in the video file myself.

This situation reminds me of the way certain creators like to hide things in their own work as a way to stake their claim to it. Sometimes these marks are things that might never be seen again, like a construction worker writing his name on a two-by-four, only to see it get covered over when the house is built around it. Or the programmer who creates a video game, and if you dig into the code you find all sorts of signs of who was there — inside jokes, names, clues — all put there by the person who

CODED THE GAME. HE KNOWS IT'S THERE, BUT
NO ONE ELSE DOES.

YOU ALSO SEE THIS KIND OF THINKING IN
EASTER EGGS, WHERE THE CREATORS OF A
VIDEO GAME WILL BUILD IN SECRET TRICKS
THAT ALLOW YOU TO MOVE FASTER, GAIN
MORE LIVES, OR OTHERWISE HACK THE GAME.
THE SAME THING CAN BE DONE WITH A VIDEO.
IF YOU WANT TO SPLICE HIDDEN THINGS INTO A
VIDEO IT'S NOT DIFFICULT TO DO. ONE FRAME
MOVES FASTER THAN THE HUMAN EYE CAN SEE,
SO WHILE YOU DON'T CONSCIOUSLY SEE THAT
SORT OF THING, YOU MIGHT SUBCONSCIOUSLY
SEE IT PASSING BY.

THE OTHER REASON THIS VIDEO SORT OF
BOTHERED ME IS THAT IT MADE ME REALIZE
HOW METICULOUS AND FOCUSED PAUL WAS. HE
TOOK THE TIME TO SCRUB THROUGH THOSE
GLITCHES, LOOKING FOR A CLUE. OR MAYBE

HE DIDN'T. WHY THIS VIDEO GLITCH AND NOT OTHERS? COULD IT BE BECAUSE HE PUT IT THERE?

THE REST OF THE VIDEO IS ONE OF THE VIDEOS FROM THE PROJECT IN PRE-PRODUCTION. HE SEES SARAH RUNNING ACROSS THE DREDGE, DROPPING THE CAMERA, THEN SLOWS DOWN THE FIRST SIGHTING OF OLD JOE BUSH. I LOVE THAT HE SLOWED IT WAY, WAY DOWN. I THINK PAUL CHANDLER'S VERSION OF THIS FOOT MOVING INTO THE FRAME IS MORE EFFECTIVE THAN THE WAY I DID IT. PROPS.

THE LAST THING I'LL MENTION ABOUT THIS VIDEO IS WHAT HE SAYS AT THE END. HE CLAIMS HE'S GOING TO TRY AND CONTACT ME, BUT TO MY KNOWLEDGE HE NEVER DID. ALTHOUGH, TO BE FAIR, I GET A LOT OF FAN MAIL AND A PARTICULARLY LARGE AMOUNT OF INQUIRY ABOUT SKELETON CREEK. IT COULD

BE THAT PAUL WAS CONTACTING ME THROUGH
SEVERAL MADE UP SOURCES, ASKING RANDOM
QUESTIONS ABOUT THIS MATERIAL. I DO RECALL
GETTING A LOT OF EMAILS AROUND THE TIME
THAT PAUL'S SITE WENT LIVE, AND THEY WERE
ALL EITHER ASKING ME THE SAME QUESTIONS
OR WARNING ME ABOUT THIS GUY WHO HAD
HACKED INTO MY SERVER.

ANY ONE OF THOSE PEOPLE COULD HAVE
BEEN PAUL CHANDLER. THEY ALL COULD
HAVE BEEN PAUL. IT'S IMPOSSIBLE TO KNOW.

SPEAKING OF EASTER EGGS, LET'S TALK
ABOUT THE ONES IN SKELETON CREEK FOR A
SECOND. THERE ARE MANY!

EASTER EGGS

WWW.SARAHFINCHER.COM WAS DESIGNED TO
LOOK LIKE SARAH FINCHER HERSELF BUILT
THE SITE. THERE'S A PHOTO OF THE DREDGE

IN THE BACKGROUND ALONG WITH A PLACE TO PUT A PASSWORD. ON THE SURFACE, IT LOOKS LIKE THAT'S ALL THERE IS TO DO AT THIS SITE. BUT IF YOU START ROLLING YOUR MOUSE AROUND YOU'RE GOING TO FIND A LOT OF HIDDEN PIECES OF INFORMATION. I'M NOT GOING TO LIST THEM ALL HERE, BUT I WILL GIVE YOU SOME CLUES AND SOME TRICKS TO FINDING ALL THE HIDDEN ITEMS:

1. AT 42 MINUTES PAST ANY HOUR, ONE OF THE WINDOWS LIGHTS UP FOR FIVE MINUTES. CLICK IT!

2. THE EASTER EGGS, OR HIDDEN ITEMS, ARE DIFFERENT AT DIFFERENT TIMES. IF YOU VISIT THE SITE BETWEEN NOON AND MIDNIGHT, YOU GET ONE SET OF EASTER EGGS. VISIT THE SITE FROM MIDNIGHT TO NOON AND YOU GET A DIFFERENT SET.

3. Roll your mouse over every part of the dredge photo. There's probably more to find than you realize.

4. Everything you find will tell you more about the story or about Sarah Fincher, the character who created the story. You'll find things like her favorite movies and her favorite bands. You'll find strange videos from her collection, things that inspired her shooting style. And you'll find photos of the dredge and other places.
I love this aspect of Skeleton Creek, because if you're willing to do a little digging, you can discover more about the character and the world of the story in new and unexpected ways.

Video Number Six

Paul's sixth video is the first one where he makes a clear claim that I found some of the videos associated with the Skeleton Creek project and then added to them for my own purposes. Go watch the video and then I'll tell you what I think.

SARAHFINCHER.COM

Password:

HAWTHORNE

All of the footage from this video is pulled from early trailers and promotional items I put out right before Skeleton Creek was published. So none of these clips are things that Paul Chandler took from my site. They were readily available to anyone with access to YouTube.

He does do one thing that's astounding though: Paul takes the earlier video he downloaded from my site and checks it against the video from the actual project. In the video Paul has from earlier, Sarah isn't clearly heard at all. But in the finished video for the project, you can hear Sarah clear as day. Based on these two videos, Paul comes to the conclusion that I must have found the originals or had them given to me, then doctored them after the fact in order

TO PUT THEM TO USE IN MY STORY.

NOW I HAVE TO GIVE A LESSON IN VIDEO POST-PRODUCTION. IT WILL BE A VERY SHORT LESSON, BECAUSE IT'S A SMALL BUT IMPORTANT THING WE'RE GETTING TO THE BOTTOM OF. WHEN WE SHOOT ON LOCATION, ESPECIALLY IF IT'S OUTSIDE AND THERE ARE A LOT OF CHALLENGES WITH THE SOUND QUALITY, THE SOUND EDITING IS DONE AFTER THE SHOOTING. THIS IS TRUE IN TELEVISION AND MOVIES AND IT'S TRUE FOR SKELETON CREEK. ALL OF THE AUDIO, INCLUDING THE SOUNDS OF THE WATER AND THE CREAKING AND THE VOICES, WAS ADDED AFTER WE SHOT THE FOOTAGE. I THINK PAUL HAD AN UNFINISHED COPY OF THE VIDEO, WHICH WOULD MAKE SENSE IF IT WEREN'T FOR THE FACT THAT SOME BUT NOT ALL OF THE AUDIO WAS ADDED IN THE FILE HE DISCOVERED FIRST. BUT WE ADD AUDIO IN MANY ROUNDS, AND USUALLY THE LAST ROUND

WOULD BE THE VOICES.

THIS TURNS OUT TO BE A VIDEO THAT DOES NOT HELP PAUL CHANDLER'S CASE. HE'S SAYING I FOUND THE VIDEOS OR THEY WERE GIVEN TO ME. I'M SAYING I MADE THEM. HE'S SAYING THE STORY IS TRUE, I'M SAYING I MADE IT UP. THIS PARTICULAR PIECE OF EVIDENCE WORKS AGAINST PAUL, BECAUSE MY ANSWER ESTABLISHES A PROCESS THAT MAKES BOTH VIDEOS POSSIBLE.

ISN'T DETECTIVE WORK FUN? LET'S DO IT AGAIN.

VIDEO NUMBER SEVEN

THIS VIDEO TAKES BACK WHAT PAUL CHANDLER LOST IN TERMS OF CREDIBILITY IN THE LAST VIDEO. CHECK IT OUT AND I'LL DO THE BEST I CAN TO EXPLAIN IT. IT'S A BIGGIE.

SARAHFINCHER.COM

Password:

DOPPELGANGER

This video claims that I was in Sumpter, Oregon in 2004 and it has a document to prove it. I could go on and on about how easily Paul Chandler could simply make this evidence on his own and put it in a video. It wouldn't be very hard to make a piece of paper that says I'm planning to go somewhere. But the truth is, I did go to Sumpter, Oregon on those dates. I was there. And it wasn't so I could scout locations for Skeleton Creek. I was on a family vacation, not thinking about work at all. Which is sometimes when real inspiration strikes.

And that's what happened. The dredge from Skeleton Creek is in Sumpter, Oregon. From the moment I saw it, I wanted to tell a ghost story that was set in the Sumpter Valley dredge. I talked to a lot of locals, including the

FOREST SERVICE STAFF WHO OVERSEE THE
DREDGE PROPERTY.

THE QUESTION YOU HAVE TO ASK YOURSELF IS
THIS: DID I MEET SOMEONE IN SUMPTER WHO
TOLD ME A STORY ABOUT THE DREDGE? DID
THEY GIVE ME A JOURNAL AND A BUNCH OF
VIDEOS? AND DID I USE THAT MATERIAL AS THE
BASIS FOR THE STORY I TOLD?

I'M NOT GOING TO ANSWER THAT BECAUSE AS
I'VE ALREADY SAID, I WANT YOU TO COME TO
YOUR OWN CONCLUSION BASED ON ALL THE
EVIDENCE.

THE MOST TROUBLING ASPECT OF THIS VIDEO
ISN'T THE ITINERARY OR THE JOURNAL. IT'S
SOMETHING WAY SUBTLER THAN THAT. IF YOU
WATCH THE VIDEO AGAIN, THERE'S A POINT
WHERE HE CALLS ME PAT CARMAN INSTEAD
OF PATRICK CARMAN. I RARELY ENCOUNTER

PEOPLE I DON'T KNOW WHO CALL ME PAT. IT'S WHAT MY FRIENDS AND FAMILY CALL ME. IT'S WHAT YOU'D CALL ME IF WE WERE PALS.

AND THIS BRINGS UP A COUPLE OF VERY INTERESTING THINGS YOU HAVE TO THINK ABOUT:

1. IF I MADE THIS WHOLE SKELETON CREEK IS REAL THING UP ON MY OWN, WOULD I HAVE LET A VIDEO LIKE THIS SLIP THROUGH? WOULDN'T I HAVE BEEN THE FIRST TO SAY 'WAIT A SECOND, WE CAN'T POST THAT. HE CALLS ME PAT. NO ONE DOES THAT IF THEY DON'T KNOW ME.'

2. OR SOMETHING EVEN MORE INTERESTING MIGHT BE GOING ON HERE: THIS PERSON I'M CALLING PAUL CHANDLER IS SOMEONE WHO KNOWS ME.

OF COURSE NOW I'M CYCLING THROUGH
EVERYONE I KNOW, EVERYONE WHO WAS
ANYWHERE NEAR THE PROJECT, ANYONE WHO
WORKED ON THE VIDEOS AND I'M THINKING:
WHO WOULD HAVE ACCESS?

UNFORTUNATELY, IT'S A LOT OF DIFFERENT
PEOPLE. AT LEAST TEN. AND IF WE'RE
INCLUDING FEMALES, AT LEAST FIFTEEN
DIFFERENT PEOPLE I KNOW COULD HAVE BEEN
INVOLVED IN THIS. SOMEONE COULD HAVE
GIVEN THESE FILES TO SOMEONE OUTSIDE THE
PROJECT, SO MAYBE IT WAS JUST A MOLE.

THIS IS PROBABLY THE RIGHT TIME TO TAKE
A BREAK FROM PAUL CHANDLER'S VIDEOS AND
SHOW YOU THREE DIFFERENT VIDEOS. THESE
THREE MIGHT ALSO CHANGE YOUR MIND ABOUT
SOME OF THIS. ONE THING IT WILL DO FOR
SURE IS MAKE YOU THINK EVEN MORE ABOUT
SKELETON CREEK.

The Haunted Back Lot

The haunted back lot was an idea one of the crew members came up with and I supported. It was a chance to go behind the scenes while we filmed the second Skeleton Creek book and let cast and crew talk openly about whether or not they thought the story was real. We turned this work into a series of four videos and posted them as part of the release of the second book.

I was all for this idea, but when I saw the final product, I was a little uncomfortable with what was shot. In fact, the person who made these videos was not invited back to continue working with us. I did feel like the end result was fair and compelling stuff, so in the end I did decide to make it public.

You're asking yourself: is this the guy? Is this our Paul Chandler? Don't think it hasn't crossed my mind. But based on everything I know and the timing of the release of all the material, I don't think this is our guy. Crew member who shot the haunted back lot = Paul Chandler? I mean, it's possible. He had access to everything. But he came into the process late. He wasn't even there when we shot the videos for the first book. I'm not sure it all adds up. And anyway he denies having anything to do with it to this day.

I have a few more comments on this, but first watch this set of videos. All four of them will unlock with one password.

SARAHFINCHER.COM

Password:

TRUSTNOONE

You'll notice that people from the cast and crew are generally vague or unwilling to share information about the town and the origins of the story. At that time I did want to protect the town from getting out into the open. I didn't know how big Skeleton Creek was going to get and this was a very small community. So I had everyone sign a non-disclosure agreement that covered everything from where we were shooting to the story itself and how I came up with it.

Of course now everyone knows we shot on the Sumpter Valley dredge. That's no secret. But back then, it was something we didn't talk about.

At the end of the last video you'll find the part that made us not invite

THIS CREW MEMBER BACK. WHAT YOU SEE IS THE DIRECTOR AND I TALKING ALONE. OR AT LEAST WE THOUGHT WE WERE ALONE. THIS CREW MEMBER HAD HIDDEN A MICROPHONE NEAR US OR HAD SOME KIND OF DIRECTIONAL MIC SO HE COULD STAND FAR AWAY AND HEAR WHAT WE WERE SAYING. I DIDN'T THINK IT WAS FAIR TO TAKE OUT WHAT WE WERE SAYING ONCE WE SAW IT IN THE OVERALL SCOPE OF THE HAUNTED BACK LOT, AND I DID THINK IT WAS REALLY FUN STUFF. HERE WE ARE, THE DIRECTOR AND THE WRITER TALKING ABOUT SOMEONE ON THE CREW WHO WAS ASKING TOO MANY QUESTIONS. WE WERE NERVOUS ABOUT WHETHER OR NOT THAT PERSON HAD SIGNED THE NON-DISCLOSURE. AND WE TALKED ABOUT GETTING RID OF HIM.

I CAN NOW TELL YOU THAT THE PERSON WE WERE TALKING ABOUT WAS IN FACT THE SAME CREW MEMBER WHO SHOT THE HAUNTED BACK

Lot videos you just watched.

As I've already said, he was not invited back to work with us after this shoot.

Is he our Paul Chandler? Personally, I don't think so. But by now maybe you're starting to get the idea here: you can't trust me any more than you can trust the director, a crew member, or some random crazed fan hacking into my server.

You can only trust yourself.

Video Number Eight

Paul's eighth video is the first time he makes mention of the name Joe Bush. It's a very short video, but you have to see it before reading further. And while you're online, do what the video tells you to do. It's cool.

SARAHFINCHER.COM

Password:

OLDJOEBUSH

If you've read the books then you know who Old Joe Bush is. He's the ghost in the story. I won't give away everything about Old Joe Bush in case you haven't read all the books, but there is one thing you should know about him: he was a real guy. This seems to be one of the reasons why so many people think the story is based on real events. I made a choice to use Joe Bush because he was a real person who really did die on a dredge. That decision has fueled more speculation than I thought it would.

But Skeleton Creek is still a work of fiction. I stand by that 100%.

So why did I choose to use a real person from history associated with a real urban legend as a character in a work of fiction? I did this because I thought

IT WOULD MAKE THE BOOK MORE EXCITING TO READ. I FIGURED IF READERS FOUND OUT THAT THE GHOST WAS BASED ON AN EXISTING URBAN LEGEND ABOUT A REAL GUY, IT WOULD HEIGHTEN THE LEVEL OF MYSTERY AND DRAW READERS DEEPER INTO THE MYTHOLOGY OF THE WORLD. IT TURNS OUT I WAS RIGHT, AT LEAST IN THE CASE OF PAUL CHANDLER.

THIS WAS A VERY SHORT VIDEO, SO IT'S ALSO A VERY SHORT ENTRY. THERE'S NOT MUCH ELSE TO SAY HERE.

VIDEO NUMBER NINE

THIS VIDEO IS A RECAP THAT DOES A SHOW AND TELL OF EVERYTHING PAUL CHANDLER HAD FIGURED OUT. IT'S A GOOD ONE TO WATCH IF YOU WANT TO MAKE SURE YOU UNDERSTAND EACH PIECE OF EVIDENCE HE HAD UNCOVERED.

SARAHFINCHER.COM

Password:

TIMEENOUGHATLAST

Because this is a recap video, I won't say much about it. I would like to mention that this is the first time Paul made a concrete connection to the actual location of the dredge. Through the use of Google Earth, he was even able to show an aerial view of the dredge. Even in regular daylight, it does have a strangely haunted feeling about it.

I think this might be the first time a very big idea crossed Paul Chandler's mind. It's when he started planning to go to the dredge and see it for himself.

Video Number Ten

The tenth video from Skeleton Creek is Real begins with a look at the dredge and the book and ends with a ghost sighting that I can't explain. Watch the video, then let's see if we can figure out what's really going on.

SARAHFINCHER.COM

PASSWORD:

SARAHFINCHER

THE FRONT END OF THIS VIDEO IS A
COMPILATION OF THINGS ANYONE COULD
HAVE FOUND ON THE WEB, SO NOTHING
GROUNDBREAKING THERE. BUT THEN PAUL
TALKS ABOUT ANOTHER FILE, ONE I DON'T
REMEMBER ANYTHING ABOUT. HE'S CLAIMING,
ONCE AGAIN, THAT HE FOUND THIS FILE ON MY
SERVER. IT'S POSSIBLE HE HACKED DEEPER
INTO THINGS THAN I FIRST REALIZED, OR
IT COULD BE THAT THIS RANDOM FILE WAS
ORPHANED ON THE SERVER AND HE FOUND A
FOLDER WHERE IT WAS HIDING. HOW SHOULD I
KNOW, I'M NOT A PROGRAMMER!

ANYWAY, I DON'T KNOW IF YOU SAW IT, BUT
I DEFINITELY SAW SOMETHING PASS THROUGH
THE DREDGE IN THAT VIDEO. TO ME IT
LOOKED LIKE SOMEONE WALKING IN A WAY
THAT WOULD INDICATE DRAGGING ONE OF THEIR
LEGS BEHIND THEM. A STEP, A PAUSE, A STEP,
A PAUSE. WATCH IT AGAIN, YOU'LL SEE WHAT

I MEAN. THIS WOULD MIMIC THE SAME TYPE OF MOVEMENTS OLD JOE BUSH WOULD MAKE, BOTH IN THE BOOKS AND IN THE URBAN LEGEND. HIS GHOST IS SAID TO WALK THIS WAY BECAUSE HIS LEG WAS CRUSHED IN THE GEARS (OR MAYBE I MADE THAT UP FOR THE BOOKS? I CAN'T REMEMBER).

I HAVE THREE POSSIBLE EXPLANATIONS FOR THIS VIDEO:

1. IT'S REAL, BUT I DON'T HAVE ANY MEMORY OF RECORDING IT OR SEEING IT PRIOR TO FINDING IT THE SKELETON CREEK IS REAL SITE.

2. I MADE IT, THEN PUT IT ON MY SITE SO PAUL CHANDLER WOULD FIND IT.

3. PAUL MADE IT HIMSELF, THEN LIED ABOUT FINDING IT ON MY SERVER.

All I can say conclusively is that whatever apparition appears in this video, it looked and felt real. I can confirm that the location is in fact the Sumpter Valley dredge, because I've been there so many times I know what that place looks like.

Paul is also beginning to talk more about going to the dredge and finding answers for himself. In the blog entry section of his site he was talking a lot about it. He was determined to visit Sumpter even in the dead of winter.

It's also clear by this time that Paul had an army of people behind him, helping him figure all this out. By this time there were over 20,000 comments on the site from thousands of different people trying to solve the same mystery he

WAS.

HERE'S ONE OF THE BLOG POSTS FROM PAUL CHANDLER. THIS WAS POSTED TO THE SITE RIGHT AROUND THE SAME TIME AS THIS VIDEO:

SORRY FOR ANOTHER WEEK WITHOUT A VIDEO BUT THINGS HAVE JUST BEEN HAPPENING TOO FAST FOR ME TO HAVE TIME TO MAKE ONE. THERE'S A LOT HAPPENING THAT I CAN'T FILL YOU IN ON YET BUT EXPECT BIG NEWS IN THE NEXT COUPLE DAYS. AT THIS POINT I CAN TELL YOU THIS: I'M GOING TO THE DREDGE SOONER THAN I THOUGHT, PROBABLY BEFORE THE END OF THE MONTH. THERE'S A LOT I STILL HAVE TO GET DONE BUT I DO KNOW I'M GOING ONE WAY OR THE OTHER. THIS WHOLE THING IS GETTING SO MUCH BIGGER AND WEIRDER THAN I EVER IMAGINED, AND I HAVE A FEELING THAT THE MORE WE FIND OUT THE MORE LIKELY SOMEBODY IS GOING TO

GET TO THE DREDGE BEFORE ME AND HIDE OR DESTROY WHATEVER I MIGHT FIND. First things first though, I need to get myself a camera...

And another blog post RIGHT AROUND THAT TIME:

So I'm sick, that kind of sick that makes you feel like you got run over by something every time you wake up. Talk about the worst time to get sick, but I suppose that's what happens when you don't really sleep much. However while I won't be doing a whole lot today I can tell you that I think I have a date for my trip to the dredge, and it will be in the neighborhood of 2 to 3 weeks from now. I'll hold off telling you the exact date until I know for certain I can make it happen, there are still some things that

aren't 100% certain to work *cough*
car *cough*. Ok I'm going to go sleep
for 9 hours now.

Video Number Eleven

We're down to only four more videos
to look at, and I think it's in these last
four that we learn the most about
the guy we're calling Paul Chandler.
Video number ten shows once again how
committed to this investigation he was,
and how he was starting to use his legion
of fans to search for things. What he
finds on this video will require me to do
some explaining. Check it out.

SARAHFINCHER.COM

Password:

TALESFROMTHECRYPT

I REMEMBER THE PHOTOGRAPH BEING SHOWN IN
THIS VIDEO. I WAS TRYING TO WORK OUT THE
FINAL MECHANICS AND LAST MINUTE CHANGES
FOR THE THIRD ATHERTON BOOK. IN THE
PICTURE I'M DRAWING MORE DETAILS INTO THE
SILO ON THE DARK PLANET, THE UNFINISHED
MANUSCRIPT IS PRINTED AND SITTING ON THE
DESK. THE OLD SLIDES ON THE DESK ARE
FROM MY CHILDHOOD, SOME OF WHICH I USED
TO ESTABLISH MOOD AND CHARACTERS.

IT MAY SEEM LIKE RYAN'S JOURNAL IS THE
MOST INTERESTING THING IN THIS PHOTOGRAPH,
BUT I DON'T THINK IT IS. THE MOST
INTERESTING THING IS WHAT'S BEHIND ME. GO
WATCH THAT VIDEO AGAIN AND YOU'LL SEE
SOMETHING ELSE:

RIGHT NEXT TO THE COMPUTER ON THE DESK
AT MY BACK, STARING PAUL CHANDLER IN
THE FACE, IS THE FIRST DRAFT OF SKELETON

CREEK. SOME OF THE PAGES ARE SITTING ON THE DESK, SOME OF THE PAGES ARE ON THE EASEL, MORE PAGES ARE ON THE SCREEN. IF ONLY THIS HAD BEEN A HIGH DEFINITION SHOT, PAUL WOULD HAVE SEEN SOMETHING AMAZING. HERE I WAS, WITH RYAN McCRAY'S JOURNAL ON MY DESK, AND THE FIRST DRAFT OF SKELETON CREEK RIGHT THERE IN THE ROOM WITH ME.

IT MIGHT MAKE A PERSON WONDER WHETHER OR NOT THE JOURNAL WAS THE SOURCE MATERIAL FOR THE BOOK I WAS WRITING. AND IF THAT WERE TRUE, WHERE DID THE JOURNAL COME FROM?

THERE ARE SEVERAL POSSIBLE ANSWERS TO THAT QUESTION:

1. I GOT THE JOURNAL FROM A SOURCE IN SUMPTER, OREGON ALONG WITH THE VIDEOS

and I used this journal and the videos as material for the story I wrote.

2. I made the journal as a way to get into the character. So maybe it's an artifact I wrote in to get inside the head of Ryan McCray for my story. Then I staged this photograph and put it on the web in an old touring photo album.

3. There never was a journal to begin with. Paul Chandler made a fake one and inserted it into this photo. If you can use Photoshop, you could do this without that much practice. Not that I'd know.

Getting back to the journal, I can tell you two things for sure and I promise you I'm telling the truth:

1. One way or another, the journal is

REAL. INSIDE, THERE ARE WORDS WRITTEN BY RYAN McCRAY. IS IT THE FICTIONAL RYAN McCRAY I CREATED, OR A REAL RYAN McCRAY WHO GAVE IT TO ME? I'M NOT GOING TO SAY.

2. I STILL HAVE THIS JOURNAL IN MY POSSESSION. IT EXISTS. I'M LOOKING AT IT RIGHT NOW.

PAUL CHANDLER ALSO PROVIDES A DATE WHEN HE'LL BE GOING UP TO THE DREDGE: DECEMBER 21ST. I THOUGHT ABOUT GOING UP THERE SO I'D SEE HIM AT THE SAME TIME HE WAS THERE, BUT IT WAS WINTER AND THERE WAS A LOT OF SNOW IN THE MOUNTAINS AT THAT TIME.

ONE THING IS CLEAR: PAUL CHANDLER WAS OBSESSED WITH FIGURING THIS OUT. CONSIDER THE EVIDENCE SO FAR, ASSUMING IT'S ALL

TRUE:

1. He hacked into my server and took things.

2. He scoured the web for information.

3. He started a web site and enlisted the help of thousands of people.

4. He made the fateful decision to drive up to the dredge in the dead of winter.

Or maybe he lives in Sumpter, Oregon and he's making that part up. Hard to know.

I'd like to say I went up there and confronted him, but I'm not going to say that. At least not yet. It's another one of those details I'm not sure I'm ready to

GIVE UP.

Video Number Twelve

This is a short video but it's worth checking out. It shows Paul Chandler getting ready to leave for the dredge. I'm guessing this was literally right before he got in his car and took off. Kind of chilling, in its own way.

SARAHFINCHER.COM

Password:

CUJO

I'M STRUCK BY THE FACT THAT HE WAS VERY CAREFUL NOT TO SHOW HIS FACE IN THE MIRROR, ONLY THE CAMERA. HE GIVES US A LOOK AT THE AUDIO SYSTEM HE'S GOING TO USE SO WE CAN HEAR HIM BETTER ONCE HE GETS GOING, HE PACKS HIS BAG, HE THINKS ABOUT RYAN McCRAY.

I HAVE TO WONDER AT THIS POINT WHAT HE EXPECTED TO ACHIEVE BY GOING UP THERE AT NIGHT IN THE FREEZING COLD. I MEAN, I'VE BEEN IN THE DREDGE PLENTY OF TIMES. THERE'S NO EVIDENCE UP THERE HE COULDN'T HAVE FOUND IN OTHER WAYS.

YOU KNOW WHAT I THINK? I THINK HE HOPED HE'D FIND RYAN McCRAY UP THERE. I THINK HE HOPED THAT RYAN HAD BEEN WATCHING THE SKELETON CREEK IS REAL SITE. IN FACT, I THINK THE SITE WAS ONLY EVER REALLY MADE FOR RYAN TO SEE.

Let's get to the thirteenth video, when we arrive on the dredge at the stroke of midnight.

Video Number Thirteen

At over eight minutes, this is by far the longest video of them all. But it might also be one of the most interesting. Seeing this guy make the trip up there and then enter the dredge is great stuff. But the best part is the end, and it's the part we're going to talk about next. Go watch! This will really get you wondering what the heck is going on.

SARAHFINCHER.COM

Password:

BERZERK

This video shows a little bit of footage on the way up to the dredge and it's obviously a desolate road in winter. He's out in the middle of nowhere, and it does look very much like the way up to the dredge.

When we first see him on the dredge, Paul says he's not going to tell us how he got in because he doesn't want to implicate anyone who might have helped him. It sounds like he may have gotten some help from someone who lives in Sumpter, or maybe he's making that up. I do know that they keep the dredge locked, so he would have had to break in or be let in by someone else.

I can verify from everything he's seeing that this is in fact the Sumpter Valley dredge. This is where we shot footage

FOR SKELETON CREEK. AND IT'S TRUE THE DREDGE HAS MANY LEVELS. IT'S ALSO SUPER CONFUSING TO NAVIGATE, ESPECIALLY AT NIGHT. THE FACT THAT HE GETS LOST IN THE DREDGE IS BELIEVABLE.

THE SOUNDS HE HEARS MIRROR THOSE THAT WE USED IN THE VIDEOS WE MADE: THE STRANGE TAPPING NOISE LIKE MORSE CODE, THE SOUND OF A FOOT BEING DRAGGED, THE WATER SOUNDS — THOSE ARE ALL DIRECTLY FROM MY WORK ON SKELETON CREEK. EITHER THE DREDGE REALLY IS HAUNTED BY THE GHOST OF OLD JOE BUSH, OR PAUL CHANDLER INSERTED THOSE SOUNDS INTO HIS VIDEO AFTER THE FACT.

BUT THE BIGGEST QUESTION THIS VIDEO RAISES IS WHO DID PAUL CHANDLER MEET AT THE END? HE DOESN'T SAY, BUT HE DOES REACT AS IF HE KNOWS THIS PERSON. THERE ARE

ONLY THREE ANSWERS THAT MAKE ANY SENSE:

1. HE SEES SOMEONE HE KNOWS, POSSIBLY RYAN McCRAY.

2. HE SEES NO ONE. HE'S ONLY ACTING LIKE HE SAW SOMEONE.

3. HE SEES ME.

I HAVE TO ADMIT, THE THIRD OPTION DOES MAKE THE MOST SENSE. HE WOULD KNOW WHAT I LOOKED LIKE. HE WOULD THINK I WAS EITHER CONCERNED FOR HIM OR ABOUT HIM. AND MAYBE, ALL ALONG, HE WAS HOPING I WAS PAYING ATTENTION AND WOULD SHOW UP TO SEE HIM. FANS HAVE DONE CRAZIER THINGS TO MEET THEIR FAVORITE AUTHOR. MAYBE IT WORKED.

BUT I'M STICKING TO MY STORY ON THIS ONE:

I THOUGHT ABOUT GOING UP THERE ON THIS
VERY NIGHT, BUT I DID NOT.

Video Number Fourteen

This is the last video from the
Skeleton Creek is Real site. If you've
stayed with me this far, then this video
will really pay off. When you come
to the end, you'll have a lot to think
about. I know I did.

SARAHFINCHER.COM

Password:

HEROBRINE

This video, and in many ways the entire experience, brings up more questions than answers. It forces you to think critically about truth and fiction, and in no place is that more true than after watching this last video.

Video number fourteen.

The one where our narrator finally tells us who he is. We can stop using the stand in name Paul Chandler. That name is dead to us now.

He's told us who he is.

He's Ryan McCray.

Or so he says.

Let's examine the scenarios this brings up.

1. The person who created this experience really is Ryan McCray. If this is true, then in many ways he was unreliable from the beginning. He talked about finding out the truth, but he knew the truth all along. The videos are his, the journal is his, he knew everything all along. And whether he manufactured some of the evidence or not, he was somehow involved from the start.

2. He's lying. This could be an elaborate creation, a world of someone's own making, a narrative of one's own. This could just be a story someone came up with and we'll never know who the real Ryan McCray is.

3. It's possible I created this experience in order to deepen the legend behind the story. But it would have been an awful lot of work to pull this off over a long period of time. Still, it's possible.

I can tell you that I have in fact met Ryan McCray. The question you have to ask yourself is in what way did I meet him? In person or in my head? The characters I write about become real, sometimes more real than people themselves. The imagination is a powerful thing.

I have met him. I think I will meet him again.

We come to the end

When it's all said and done we come full circle, back to the beginning:
Urban legends are as real as our imaginations choose to make them.
Maybe the real question this book answers is not whether Skeleton Creek is real, but how big your imagination is. Part of my job as a writer is to never break the spell. Even if I did know the whole truth, I wouldn't tell you.

Here are just a few of the ways you might interpret what you've just experienced, based solely on the shape and size of something that belongs only to you — your imagination.

The author made all of this up. He is the unreliable narrator. He alone knows the

TRUTH, AND HE WILL NEVER TELL.

RYAN McCRAY AND SARAH FINCHER, OR
SOME VERSIONS OF THEM, ARE REAL. IT
IS THEY WHO TOLD THIS STORY TO ME.
I CHANGED THEIR STORY FOR MY OWN
PURPOSES, BUT THERE IS REAL TRUTH HERE.

THE PERSON WHO MADE SKELETON CREEK
IS REAL MADE IT ENTIRELY FROM HIS OWN
IMAGINATION. IT IS A COMPLETE HOAX.

LIKE THE BEST URBAN LEGENDS, THIS ONE
HAS PARTS AND PIECES YOU CAN NEVER FULLY
KNOW. IT'S LIKE A BOX YOU HAVEN'T OPENED.
WHAT'S INSIDE IS IMPOSSIBLE TO SEE, BUT IF
YOU SHAKE IT AROUND, IF YOU LISTEN, IF YOU
FEEL ITS WEIGHT — YOU CAN GUESS AT ITS
CONTENTS.

ONCE THE BOX IS OPENED THE SPELL IS

BROKEN. IT WILL NEVER HAVE THE SAME POWER OVER YOUR IMAGINATION ONCE YOU SEE THE INSIDE.

AND SO IT IS WITH US. I LEAVE YOU NOW WITH A DECISION TO MAKE, AND IT IS YOURS AND YOURS ALONE. THIS DECISION DOES NOT BELONG TO ME. YOU MUST ANSWER THIS QUESTION FOR YOURSELF.

IS SKELETON CREEK REAL?

ONLY YOU CAN SAY.

BECAUSE I'LL NEVER TELL.

Additional Fan Theories

I had a chance to read through all of the 30,000 plus comments that were left on the Skeleton Creek is Real site. Here, for posterity, are some of the theories those fans came up with.

Posted by SCIRarmy

Ok, someone on this website said that Joe Bush and George Bush are related. Well, probably not but Joe Bush could be based off of George Bush. I mean even though some things are different the main person itself could have been based on George Bush coz he was part of the Freemasons. We need evidence that tells us if it 100% true or not.

Posted by That Person Over There Eating With Chopsticks

The Crossbones was an old crime group

WHO HAD ONE OF THEIR MEMBERS (JOE BUSH) TRY TO STEAL GOLD FROM A GOLD DREDGE. HE DIED THIS WHILE ON THE JOB. JOE BUSH KEPT A JOURNAL THAT HE USED TO KEEP INFO ON THE OTHER GUARDS AND TO PLAN HIS ROBBERY. SOMETIME LATER HIS NEPHEW RYAN AND HIS NIECE SARAH FOUND HIS JOURNAL.

POSTED BY AMANDA H.

I HAVE A FEELING THAT THE NEW CROSSBONES IS US. IT SEEMS CRAZY AT FIRST...BUT TRY AND THINK ABOUT IT. WE. ARE. THE CROSSBONES.

POSTED BY KAILEE G.

THE MORSE CODE WE FOUND IS THE SAME CODE THEY USED ON THE TITANIC TO SEND MESSAGES. IN THE EARLIER DAYS THE FIRST TELEGRAPH SENT MESSAGES BY TAPPING ON STUFF, AND THE CODE IS THE SAME AS THE

ONE WE FOUND. I FOUND THIS OUT BY BUYING A BOOK FROM THE TOWN LIBRARY.

Posted by Thesymbolicwolf42

I THINK RYAN, SARAH AND JOE BUSH ARE REAL PEOPLE. AND THERE ARE SECRETS THAT ARE SO DARK AND POWERFUL THAT PEOPLE WANT THEM TO STAY BURIED. BUT THINGS CANNOT STAY BURIED OR FORGOTTEN. HERE IS AN IDEA: MAYBE PATRICK CARMAN IS PART OF THE CROSSBONES BECAUSE HE KNOWS A LOT ABOUT EDGAR ALLEN POE. CARMAN IS PART OF THE GROUP BECAUSE THEY FEAR HIM AND HIS WORDS.

Posted by Spades

IF YOU CLICK ON THE DICE EASTER EGG, IT HAS A PICTURE OF DICE WITH THE NUMBERS 3, 1 AND 5. SO THAT CONFIRMS THE 315 STORIES ARE MOST DEFINITELY CONNECTED TO THE DREDGE.

AUTHOR NOTE: 3:15 IS ANOTHER SERIES I WROTE WITH AUDIO AND VIDEO FILES. FIND IT AT WWW.315STORIES.COM. THE DICE EASTER EGG IS AT WWW.SARAHFINCHER.COM. CLICK ALL THE LOWER WINDOWS, LEFT TO RIGHT, AND THE VIDEO WILL PLAY. THE SONG WAS WRITTEN AND PERFORMED BY SOME FRIENDS OF MINE.

POSTED BY SUPERSECRET

WHY DO I HAVE A FEELING THAT THE SARAH (THE REAL ONE) IS ACTING AS THE APOSTLE? MAYBE THE NEW CROSSBONES ARE ALREADY AMONG US?

POSTED BY ALEXRIDER7

IN BOOK 4 (THE RAVEN) RYAN SAYS THAT HE, SARAH, AND FITZ ARE THE CROSSBONES NOW. I BELIEVE IT WAS BETWEEN BOOK 3 AND BOOK 4 THAT PATRICK GAVE US HIS VIDEO RESPONSE TO THIS WEBSITE. THEN, BOOK

4 HE DECIDED TO END SARAH AND RYAN'S SEARCH IN THE TOWN THEY LIVE IN. AND IS IT ME, OR DID SARAH'S VOICE CHANGE BETWEEN BOOK 3 N 4 ? ? ? HMMM.

POSTED BY CJSAWESOME

I THINK PATRICK CARMAN FOUND THE VIDEOS AND REENACTED THEM.

POSTED BY NUDGEGIRL

I FOUND SOME STUFF ON OLD JOE BUSH. HE HAS TWO POSSIBLE IDENTITIES FROM WKIPEDIA:

JOE BUSH IS THE NAME OF A GHOST THAT ALLEGEDLY HAUNTS THE SUMPTER VALLEY GOLD DREDGE IN SUMPTER, OREGON, UNITED STATES. DREDGE WORKERS WORKING ON THE No. 3 DREDGE AT SUMPTER VALLEY OFTEN REPORTED STRANGE HAPPENINGS INVOLVING THE GHOST. THE GHOST IS SAID TO LEAVE WET, BARE FOOTPRINTS ON THE DREDGE'S

DECKS AND CAUSE LIGHTS TO FLICKER AND DOORS TO OPEN AND CLOSE UNEXPECTEDLY.

THEORIES OF IDENTITY – CONTROVERSY SURROUNDS JOE BUSH'S ACTUAL IDENTITY. THERE ARE TWO MAIN THEORIES:

1. CHRIS ROWE WORKED ON THE No. 1 DREDGE AS AN OILER MAINTAINING THE GEARBOX. IN 1918 HE WAS INEXPLICABLY CRUSHED IN THE GEARS THAT HE WORKED ON WHILE ON DUTY. NO ONE WAS PRESENT AND AN EXPLANATION NEVER DEVELOPED. WHEN THE GEARS FROM THE No. 1 DREDGE WERE TRANSFERRED TO THE No. 3, THE ONE THAT STILL STANDS IN SUMPTER VALLEY DREDGE STATE PARK, CHRIS ROWE'S GHOST TRAVELED WITH THE GEARBOX. THE PROBLEM IS THAT REPORTS OF THE GHOST WERE NEVER REPORTED ON THE No. 1 DREDGE.

2. WHILE DOCUMENTATION DOES NOT EXIST

FOR THE EMPLOYMENT OF ANYONE NAMED
JOE BUSH, FORMER WORKERS SAID THERE WAS
A MECHANIC NAMED JOE BUSH ON THE No.
49 DREDGE DURING ITS OPERATING YEARS. HE
WAS EMPLOYED FOR A FEW YEARS BUT MAY
HAVE PROVIDED AN ALTERNATE NAME FOR
EMPLOYMENT RECORDS.

POSTED BY KILLER NINJA

IN ONE OF THE BOOKS WE FIND OUT THAT
JOE BUSH (THE REAL GHOST) IS ACTUALLY A
GOOD GUY AND THAT THE REAL CROSSBONES IS
DEFERENT THEN THE SUMPTER CROSSBONES.
WELL HERE'S WHAT I THANK — JOE BUSH WAS
PART OF THE REAL CROSSBONES WITH THE
"GHOST" THE "RAVEN" AND THE "APOSTLE".
JOE FIGURED OUT THAT THE CROSSBONES
WERE BAD NEWS SO HE FLED TO SUMPTER
AND CHANGED HIS NAME TO JOE BUSH. THE
RAVEN FIGURED OUT HE WAS THERE FINDING
GOLD. THE RAVEN WANTED THAT GOLD SO HE

SENT THE APOSTLE AFTER HIM. WHILE JOE
WORKED ON THE DREDGE HE FIGURED THAT
THEY WOULD COME SO HE MADE A SECRET
ROOM WITH THE SUMPTER CROSSBONES
MEMBERS IN IT. WHEN THE APOSTLE FOUND
JOE HE "ACCIDENTLY" SHOVED HIM IN THE
WATER TO HIS DEATH. THE GHOST AKA HENRY
FIGURED THIS OUT YEARS LATER AND KILLED
THE APOSTLE SEARCHING FOR THE GOLD.

POSTED BY THE REAPER

HERE IS WHAT I THINK IS GOING ON. RYAN'S
DAD AND THE REST OF THE CROSSBONES ARE
PART OF A SECRET SOCIETY THAT STEAL GOLD
FROM THE DREDGE COMPANY ASSET #42,
AND THEY KEPT THEIR GOLD IN A ROOM HIDDEN
INSIDE THE DREDGE.

I THINK HENRY, AS THE OWNER, HELPED THEM
SMUGGLE GOLD AWAY FROM THE DREDGE
BUT OLD JOE BUSH WAS GOING TO REPORT

THE GROUP, SO HE GRABBED AS MUCH GOLD
AS HE COULD, SHOVED IT IN HIS POCKETS AND
WAS GOING TO RUN FOR IT WHEN ONE OF THE
MEMBERS FIGURED OUT WHAT HE WAS DOING
AND SHOVED HIM INTO THE MACHINE, THUS
KILLING HIM.

THAT IS WHY RYAN'S FATHER SEEMED SO
PREJUDICE AGAINST JOE BUSH WHEN HE WAS
TELLING HIS SON ABOUT HIM.

THE COMPANY MUST HAVE CAUGHT UP WITH
THE CRIMINALS SO THEY DECIDED TO STAY
LOW FOR A WHILE, BUT THEN THE COMPANY
WAS DEMOLISHED SO THE DREDGE NO LONGER
PICKED UP GOLD, SO THE GROUP WAS CALLED
OFF.

THIS EXPLAINS WHY RYAN'S FATHER WANTS
SARAH AWAY FROM RYAN, NOT FOR SAFETY
BUT HE IS AFRAID HE AND SARAH WILL

DISCOVER HIS CRIMINAL PAST AND THE
AUTHORITIES WILL HEAR ABOUT IT AND ARREST
HIM, HE SEEMS A BIT TOO EAGER TO MOVE
IF RYAN IS MAKING CONTACT WITH SARAH.

I AM SORRY IF MY PREDICTION IS PROVED
WRONG IN THE SECOND BOOK, I HAVE JUST
FINISHED BOOK 1, ABOUT HALF AN HOUR AGO,
AND I INTEND TO GO TO THE LIBRARY AND GET
BOOK 2 TOMORROW.

POSTED BY SGTSTEALTH

MY THEORY: RYAN'S DAD WORKED ON THE
DREDGE WITH JOE BUSH (HIS "SUPPOSED"
NAME). JB HEARD ABOUT THE SECRET
SOCIETY, AND ASKED ONE TOO MANY
QUESTIONS. THE ALCHEMIST (RYAN'S DAD?)
PUSHED JOE BUSH INTO THE GEARS. THEN
JOE COMES BACK FROM THE DEAD FOR EITHER
A) THE "GOLD" THAT THE SOCIETY HAS, B)

REVENGE AGAINST THE ALCHEMIST, OR C)
BOTH.

POSTED BY JBILL

PATRICK CARMAN VISITED THE DREDGE AND
TALKED TO SOMEONE WHILE HE WAS THERE.
THEY TOLD HIM THERE WAS THIS URBAN
LEGEND ABOUT A GHOST AND GAVE HIM THE
NAME OF SOMEONE WITH THE INITIALS RM
WHO LIVED SOMEWHERE AROUND THE AREA.
RM GAVE CARMAN A JOURNAL WITH NOTES
FROM HIM AND HIS GIRLFRIEND TRYING TO GET
IN THE DREDGE AT NIGHT AND FILM SOMETHING
SCARY. RYAN KEPT A JOURNAL AND HIS
GIRLFRIEND TAPED ALL THE VIDS.

THEN THE GIRL DISAPPEARED OR DIED OR
SOMETHING AND RM WENT A LITTLE NUTS.
RM THINKS THE GHOST IS REAL, TELLS
PATRICK CARMAN THE WHOLE STORY, GIVES
HIM A BUNCH OF RECORDED STUFF FROM HIS

GIRLFRIEND, WHICH TOTALLY GETS HER MAD
AND SHE BREAKS UP WITH HIM — OR SHE'S
ALREADY DEAD OR GONE LIKE I SAID.

RM ASKS FOR HIS STUFF BACK BUT BY THEN
IT'S TOO LATE. BY THEN PATRICK CARMAN
IS INTO IT. MAYBE HE EVEN BELIEVES THERE
ACTUALLY IS A GHOST AND HE SPENDS THE
NIGHT UP THERE AND GETS FREAKED OUT. HE
WATCHES THE VIDEOS FROM RM'S GIRLFRIEND,
READS THE JOURNAL, WRITES UP AN OUTLINE
FOR A PROJECT THAT'S A BOOK AND VIDEOS
ALL MASHED UP TOGETHER AND SELLS IT TO
SCHOLASTIC FOR BIG BUCKS. WHERE'S THE
GIRLFRIEND? WHERE'S RM? WHY HAVEN'T
WE HEARD FROM THEM? MAYBE THEY
GOT PAID ENOUGH TO LET IT GO OR MAYBE
THEY'RE SCARED. THEY PROBABLY GOT OUT
OF THAT PLACE IF THEY GOT SCARED ENOUGH
AND DIDN'T WANT TO HANG AROUND ANYMORE.
I BET RYAN WISHED HE NEVER GAVE UP THE

TAPES OR THE JOURNAL.

POSTED BY HELPSCAREDWOLDGIRL

WHEN DREDGE #3 WAS INDUCTED INTO THE FLEET IN 1934 IT WAS HOPED THAT SUMPTER WOULD PROSPER MORE THAN EVER. THE MINERS WORKING UNDERGROUND WERE FINDING MORE GOLD THAN THE ENORMOUS DREDGES; DREDGE WORKERS WERE NERVOUS FOR THEIR JOBS.

JOE BUSH REPORTEDLY DIED WHILE TRYING TO REPAIR ONE OF THE GEAR MECHANISMS WHILE THE DREDGE WAS STILL IN OPERATION BECAUSE HE DIDN'T WANT TO HALT THE SEARCH FOR GOLD.

TWENTY YEARS AFTER DREDGE #3 (ONE OF ITS MANY NAMES) BEGAN ITS WORK, IT WAS HALTED. AND HAUNTED. WET FOOTPRINTS ON THE DECK, STRANGE SOUNDS, MISSING OBJECTS.

The ghost-like visions and eerie sounds are said to be the work of Joe Bush. Apparently his good intentions to save the mining company time and money led to his unsettling death — which he has not forgotten nor forgiven.

Posted by marshmallow milkshake

I was online reading the newspaper article of the Casper Star Tribune for March 1, 2004 about Oregon's Sumpter Valley gold dredge and a man thinks he had an encounter with a Bigfoot/Sasquatch in the area. Could Bigfoot be involved in the strange goings on in Skeleton Creek??? The Pacific Northwest has many legends about them.

Posted by horror

I have an idea about who the alchemist is. A long time ago there was a guy named

Nicholas Flamel who was called the alchemist. He was the best alchemist of his time. It is said that he bought a book that told how to make the philosophers stone. It could turn metal into gold and give immortality. What if the Crossbones know where the book and the philosopher's stone are and Joe bush found out so the Crossbones murdered him?

Posted by Boo007

You know I was thinking that maybe Patrick Carman lived in Sumpter, OR. He's just telling a story from his childhood. Maybe it happened to him when he was young or it happened to a friend but researching all of this leads to dead ends. He might be able to delete videos but he can't delete books out of a library can he?

WE ALL KNOW THAT PATRICK CARMAN IS
COVERING UP THE TRUE STORY. THE REAL
QUESTION WE SHOULD BE ASKING IS WHY?

WOULDN'T IT MAKE MORE SENSE TO SELL
THIS OFF AS A TRUE STORY? THERE WOULD
BE MORE MONEY IN IT THAT WAY, HE COULD
USE THE ACTUAL VIDEOS AND MAKE THE BOOK
THAT MUCH MORE REALISTIC. SO WHY WOULD
HE SELL IT ALL AS FAKE, WHY WOULD HE
REMAKE THE MOVIES?

MY FIRST THEORY IS THAT THE CHARACTERS
JUST WEREN'T DYNAMIC ENOUGH. THE STORY
OF RYAN AND SARAH IS SETTLED RIGHT FROM
THE GET-GO AND SEEMS VERY CHARGED
ALREADY. BUT WHAT IF THE CHARACTERS WERE
LACKING FROM A WRITER'S PERSPECTIVE?
A BOOK WITH A GOOD STORY AND BAD
CHARACTERS IS MEDIOCRE. NO AUTHOR WANTS

TO WRITE AN OKAY NOVEL. SO BY USING THE NORMAL FOOTAGE AS A REFERENCE, MR. CARMAN CREATES MORE DYNAMIC CHARACTERS. IF YOU HAVE WATCHED THE VIDEO AT SARAHFINCHER.COM, YOU MIGHT BE ABLE TO SEE WHAT I'M TALKING ABOUT. SOME OF IT JUST SEEMS TO WELL DONE.

MY SECOND THEORY, THE ONE I HOPE IS INCORRECT:

SOMETHING BAD HAPPENED TO RYAN AND SARAH. SOMETHING THAT WOULD SELL BETTER IF IT WAS LABELED AS FICTION.

POSTED BY MUTANTBIRDKID

SKELETON CREEK IS REAL. WHEN THE BOOK CAME OUT, I JUST THOUGHT IT WOULD BE A GOOD READ, BUT AS I READ IT, IT BROUGHT BACK AN ENGLISH ASSIGNMENT FROM ABOUT 2003. WE WERE DOING A NEWSPAPER, AND

I WAS THE EDITOR. SOMEONE WAS WRITING ABOUT HOW TWO KIDS FROM SUMPTER, OREGON HAD GOTTEN IN TROUBLE BECAUSE THEY WERE ON A DREDGE AT NIGHT AND ONE OF THEM GOT HURT. THE KID'S NAMES WERE RYAN AND SARAH! AND RYAN, THE ONE WHO GOT HURT, WAS UNCONSCIOUSLY MUTTERING SOMETHING ABOUT A GHOST AND OLD JOE BUSH.

POSTED BY OBLIVION

I HAVE FOUND SOMETHING COMPLETELY REMARKABLE AFTER DOING RESEARCH FOR THE NEXT BOOK: GHOST IN THE MACHINE. I DID A FEW SEARCHES ON GOOGLE AND CAME UP WITH A BOOK FROM THE 1960s, WHICH WAS AT THE TIME WHEN RUSSIA WAS THE USSR. AS WE ALL KNOW THERE IS A VIDEO ON THE SITE ITSELF WITH VIDEOS FROM THAT TIME BUT DID ANYONE EVER RECOGNIZE THE SYMBOLS ON THAT DOOR ON THE FLOOR IN THE SECRET

ROOM? THE TWO SYMBOLS ON EACH SIDE
OF THE BONES ARE ON THE USSR FLAG. SO
THAT LED ME INTO LOOKING AT THIS BOOK
I FOUND EVEN MORE. IT'S CALLED GHOST IN
THE MACHINE. I FOUND ANOTHER BOOK CALLED
FLESH TO METAL WHICH STARTS OFF TALKING
ABOUT HOW THE RUSSIANS WANTED TO BUILD
THEIR MEN LIKE METAL SO THAT THEY WOULD
BE "ROCK HARD" MEN AND GOOD SOLDIERS.

YOU PROBABLY WANT TO KNOW WHERE I'M
GOING WITH THIS...WELL I'VE BEEN THINKING
ABOUT IT AND MY THEORY IS THAT AFTER
THE DEATH OF JOE BUSH, THE CROSSBONES
NEEDED TO BRING HIM BACK SO THEY TRIED
TO RECREATE HIM BY MAKING HIM OUT OF
METAL. THEY USED HIS OWN BODY, BUT PUT
METAL PARTS INSIDE TO MAKE HIM WORK
AGAIN, SORT OF LIKE A ROBOT. THE ONLY
PROBLEM IS THAT HIS SOUL CAME BACK INTO
THE BODY AND EVER SINCE THEN HE STAYED

IN THE DREDGE, KEEPING EVERYONE AWAY.
THAT'S WHY HE LOOKS THE WAY HE DOES, IT'S
BECAUSE HIS FLESH IS NO LONGER THERE AND
HIS BODY IS NOTHING MORE THAN A WALKING
SKELETON.

POSTED BY HYYPUR

MY THEORY IS THAT IT IS ALL REAL AND THAT
RYAN'S DAD IS THE ALCHEMIST. YOU CAN
TELL BECAUSE HE HAS THAT ALCHEMY SYMBOL
FOR GOLD ON HIS ARM, AND YOU CAN SEE THE
SYMBOL SEVERAL TIMES THROUGHOUT THE
BOOK VIDEOS.

POSTED BY SKELETONCREEK1234

IF SUMPTER IS A LOT LIKE SKELETON
CREEK, THEN OF COURSE THIS IS BASED OFF
OF A TRUE STORY. THINK ABOUT IT, THIS
GUY PATRICK CARMAN IS DEFINITELY HIDING
SOMETHING.

Posted by Jill

I think there's some sort of split personality going on. What if the guy running this site went to the dredge and when he says at the end 'what are you doing here?' there wasn't anyone there? It could be an alter-ego or figment of his imagination. It could be all of this has been created but not by the author, by someone else.

Posted by Zack

Patrick Carman knows more than we think guys. My theory.... He is up to something big. He knows Ryan McCray, he's got to know him. I mean c'mon he's got notebooks all throughout his pics. He has something up his sleeve and we need to find out what it is.

I have a theory. I think the RM diary is the book itself (cleaned up of course.) I also think the guy who owns the Skeleton Creek is Real site is trying to throw us off the trail with the stuff that was recently found in the phantom file. Guys I think the RM diary may be fake but the location is defiantly fake. For all we know the videos that were taken are somewhere else entirely. But if the RM diary does exist it would be a gold mine of info. I think it's also possible that whoever RM is he's dead. He and the girl both. Or maybe he's dead and she freaked out, left the tapes and the journal for her favorite author and went silent. That'd be wild. Could be.

DISCUSSION GUIDE

What you have just experienced would make a good basis for a discussion with friends, teachers, students, librarians, or anyone else willing to listen. You have a lot of information in the form of words and videos. You have conducted an investigation into truth and fiction, and you have not been handed the answers you seek. If you're an educator, the following discussion guide might make for a riveting class conversation. If you have friends who have also read and watched this material, these are the kinds of questions you should be asking yourself.

I. Unreliable Narrators

Skeleton Creek is Real began as a web site someone developed to explored the source material for the Skeleton Creek series of books. It was never clear whether or not this person we called Paul Chandler and Ryan McCray could be trusted. I have taken what was presented on the site and examined it from my own perspective, presenting all the information as simply and clearly as I could.

What is an unreliable narrator?

Who do you think was more reliable, me or the unidentified creator of the site?

Are there other examples of this type of storytelling in books you've read or heard of?

Does this experience make you a more critical thinker? In other words, are you more likely to question what you're reading, both on the Internet and in print?

2. Urban Legends

We've talked a lot about Urban Legends in this investigation. They appear to be powerful things that take on a life of their own. They can shape what we think and believe. They have an unusual power over us.

What is an urban legend?

Is there an urban legend in your part of the world? If so, what is it?

Do you think urban legends are usually true or false? Why?

3. Determining facts from fiction

We live in a time of unprecedented information. Every answer, it seems, is at our fingertips. But this glut of information makes it easy to believe everything we read. One of the most important things about Skeleton Creek is Real is the power it has to help you sort fact from fiction. Learning to examine information with a critical eye is more important than ever.

Have you ever read or seen a hoax on the Internet you thought was true, only to discover later that it was false? If so, what was it?

Have you ever listened to a politician and wondered if they were telling the whole truth, or only the parts they want you to hear? How does it make

YOU FEEL WHEN YOU KNOW THIS IS TAKING PLACE?

HAS ANYONE EVER SAID SOMETHING ABOUT YOU ONLINE THAT WASN'T TRUE? HOW DID YOU HELP OTHER PEOPLE DETERMINE FACT FROM FICTION WHEN THIS HAPPENED?

4. COMING TO YOUR OWN CONCLUSIONS
WHEN A SET OF CIRCUMSTANCES DOESN'T GIVE US CONCRETE ANSWERS, IT OFFERS US AN OPPORTUNITY TO THINK FOR OURSELVES. IT PROVIDES SPACE TO DEBATE OUR POINT OF VIEW, EVEN IF NO REAL ANSWER CAN EVER BE FOUND.

NOW THAT YOU'VE READ AND SEEN EVERYTHING, WHAT DO YOU BELIEVE ABOUT SKELETON CREEK?

WOULD YOU RATHER KNOW THE TRUTH, OR DO
YOU LIKE THE MYSTERY OF NOT KNOWING?

THE SKELETON CREEK BOOKS
IN ORDER TO GAIN A BETTER UNDERSTANDING
OF THIS INVESTIGATION, CONSIDER READING
THE SKELETON CREEK SERIES OF BOOKS. IN
ORDER, THE SERIES TITLES ARE:

SKELETON CREEK
GHOST IN THE MACHINE
THE CROSSBONES
THE RAVEN

PATRICK CARMAN
2014

Postscript

There is one more video that surfaced during the period of time when Skeleton Creek was being made. It found its way onto the Internet and remains there. You can find it if you search for oldiejoyfulwin, or you can watch it using the password provided below.

It's classic Ryan McCray.

SARAHFINCHER.COM

Password:

OLDIEJOYFULWIN